For Jackeline, Joel Jr., and Karen Flores
—L. K. M.

To Clementine,
who was born when I began working on this book, with love and joy.
—J. D.

Thank you to Olivier Dunrea for suggesting I use
140 lb. cold-press paper and gouache for this book, which I did.
—J. D.

Text © 2008 by Laura Krauss Melmed.
Illustrations © 2008 by Jane Dyer.

Typeset in Cantoria.
The illustrations in this book were rendered in gouache.
Manufactured in China.

Library of Congress Cataloging-in-Publication Data
Melmed, Laura Krauss.
Hurry! Hurry! Have you heard? / by Laura Krauss Melmed ; illustrated by Jane Dyer.
p. cm.
Summary: A small bird, her heart filled with love, hurries from her perch
above the manger to spread the news to creatures of the field and
forest that a child has been born to whom all are precious.
ISBN 978-0-8118-4225-9
1. Jesus Christ—Nativity—Juvenile fiction. [1. Jesus Christ—Nativity—Fiction.
2. Birds—Fiction. 3. Animals—Fiction. 4. Stories in rhyme.] I. Dyer, Jane, ill. II. Title.
PZ8.3.M55155Hur 2008
[E]—dc22
2007021062

10 9 8 7 6 5 4 3 2 1

Chronicle Books LLC
680 Second Street, San Francisco, California 94107

www.chroniclekids.com

Hurry! Hurry!
HAVE YOU HEARD?

by **LAURA KRAUSS MELMED**

illustrated by **JANE DYER**

chronicle books · san francisco

A brand-new star rose in the sky
And shone with all its might
To celebrate a baby's birth
One peaceful winter's night.

Three kittens sleeping in the straw,

All snug in downy fur,

Woke up to find the newborn boy,

And they began to purr.

A small bird nesting on a beam

Hopped down from up above,

And when the baby smiled at her,

Her heart filled up with love.

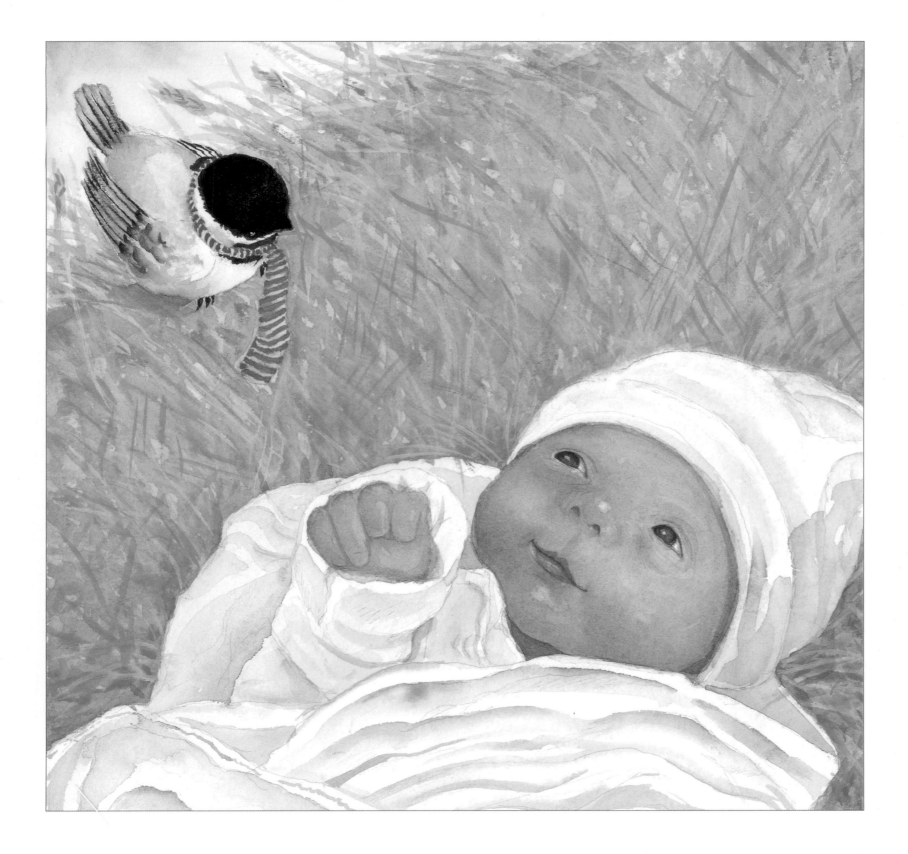

So out over the countryside

She soared on wings of joy,

Inviting friends from far and wide

To welcome the new boy.

"Hurry! Hurry! Have you heard?
A child was born tonight,
And every creature large or small
Is precious in his sight."

"Hurry, Bunny! Hurry, Fox!
He's come to bring us peace,
And just for him a special star
Has risen in the east."

"Hurry, Pup!" The pup woke up,

And with a playful leap,

He bounded off to see the babe

And brought two little sheep.

"Scurry, furry little mouse!"
  The mouse gazed at the star,
  Deciding she would go along,
  Although it might be far.

A tiny shrew called, "I'll go too!"

And scampered from his tree,

Just as mole popped from her hole,

Exclaiming, "Wait for me!"

The spider and the ladybug

And other creeping things

Joined in, while bee and hummingbird

Flew fast on whirring wings.

Last but not least, a tortoise crawled
Quite calmly, at the rear.

"I know I'm slow, but still I'll go
To wish the child good cheer."

When mole and pup and little mouse

And shrew and bumblebee

All crowded 'round the little boy,

He crowed and cooed with glee.

Then all his new friends welcomed him—

Each had a way to speak—

With yip or mew or wiggle,

With buzz or chirp or squeak.

Oh! What a noisy serenade!

The babe began to cry.

His mama took him in her arms,

And crooned a lullaby.

Then quiet, like a soft quilt, spread,

'Til not one purr or peep

Was heard from kitten, babe, or bird…

For they…were…fast…asleep!